FROZEN

STAY AWAKE...

Read
INSOMNIACS

1 ROAD KILL
2 FROZEN
3 TALK TO ME
4 TUNNEL

S.R. Martin

INSOMNIACS

FROZEN

SCHOLASTIC INC.
New York Toronto London Auckland Sydney
Mexico City New Delhi Hong Kong

No part of this publication may be reproduced in whole or in part, or stored in a retrieval system or transmitted in any form or by any means, electronic, mechanical, photocopying, recording, or otherwise, without written permission of the publisher. For information regarding permission, write to Scholastic Australia Pty Limited, ACN 000 614 577, PO Box 579, Gosford 2250, Australia.

ISBN 0-590-69141-4

Copyright © 1997 by S.R. Martin.

All rights reserved. Published by Scholastic Inc., 555 Broadway, New York, NY 10012, by arrangement with Scholastic Australia Pty Limited.

SCHOLASTIC and associated logos are trademarks and/or registered trademarks of Scholastic Inc.

12 11 10 9 8 7 6 5 4 3 2 1   9/9 0 1 2 3 4/0

Printed in the U.S.A.

First Scholastic printing, March 1999

FROZEN

1
CHAPTER ONE

Gerard had never felt cold.

Not really cold, anyway.

Sure, he'd felt cooler than normal, and had occasionally said the words, "Boy, I sure feel cold," but, in essence, he didn't honestly know what he was talking about.

You see, Gerard was born and grew up in Xanthers, and there the temperature never dropped below about 77 degrees. And that was in the middle of winter (what the people of Xanthers called winter). Most of the time it was 95+ . . . in the shade.

During summer you could fry eggs on the sidewalk, defrost a frozen chicken in the trunk of your car in five minutes, or lose those few extra pounds just by walking out to the garage at lunchtime.

Xanthers was hot.

And so was Gerard, according to most of the girls in his class. He looked a lot like a teenage Brad Pitt and had a seemingly endless wardrobe of baggy jeans, T-shirts, and baseball caps, which he wore to devastating effect. Over the last couple of years Gerard had broken more hearts in his classroom than he had pencils, and he used to boast to his friends that he could go out with any girl he wanted at their school, even the ones that were older than he was.

Apart from being good-looking, he was also captain of the school junior football team and the star batter for the local under-fourteen baseball club.

He was also arrogant, egotistical, and an absolute swine.

In short, he loved himself to death.

Gerard was thinking seriously about breaking up with his girlfriend, Stephanie (they'd been going out for two weeks already, which, for Gerard, was almost akin to being married), when a new student was introduced to their class.

It was a hot midsummer morning and the class was in turmoil. As yet their teacher, Ms. Jenkins (Gerard liked to tell his friends that she had "a thing" for him, but being in her early twenties was "much too old" for his taste), had not arrived, so the air was filled with well-aimed missiles, curses, and a general smattering of laughter.

Gerard was sitting in the back surrounded

by his usual crowd of guys, talking about the time he'd spent at the pool over the weekend and pointedly ignoring Stephanie, who was sitting at the desk to his right. No matter how hard she tried to catch his eye, Gerard simply refused to see, and the more he refused to see, the bigger Stephanie's pout became, until it seemed as if her entire bottom lip were going to flop over and cover her chin.

She was about to let fly with one of the cutting remarks she was so well known for when the door to the classroom suddenly flew open and slammed into the wall. It sounded like a rifle shot and everyone in the room froze, so when Ms. Jenkins walked through the door there were students with their mouths still wide open, arms in the air (caught in the middle of throwing something), midstep between desks, and Billy

Michaels was holding Rosco, the class nerd, in a headlock.

"Morning, class," Ms. Jenkins said briskly as she strode toward her desk. "Please take your seats. And Billy, let go of Rosco before you strangle him."

There was a loud thump as Rosco hit the floor, gasping for breath.

After a second or two of settling, the class gradually began to focus their attention on the small figure standing just inside the doorway. It was a girl, and she just seemed to have appeared there, though everyone knew she must have come inside with Ms. Jenkins.

No one, however, had noticed her at the time.

She was dressed much like everyone else, in jeans and a loose shirt, but her hair was pulled straight back from her face and braided with what appeared to be hundreds of brightly colored beads. It looked like some sort of old-fashioned hippie curtain draped across her shoulders. Her skin was a very dark mahogany and her eyes were huge and black, almost as if they were holes drilled far back into her skull.

Without question, she was the most beautiful, intriguing person Gerard had ever set eyes upon.

"I'd like you all to say hello to Sadie," Ms. Jenkins announced. "She's come to us from Haiti."

"What sort of a place is called Hate Me?" Billy whispered across to Gerard.

"Haiti, you moron," Gerard hissed back.

The class all droned out, "Hello, Sadie."

"Sadie's father is an engineer," Ms. Jenkins continued, "and they'll be here for a couple of years while the new shopping center is being built. They've taken the old Catchpole house. I'd like you all to make her feel welcome, and she'll have a lot to tell us about her country, I'm sure. You can have the desk down in front near me, Sadie, until you've settled in and worked out who you'd like to sit next to for the rest of the semester."

Gerard leaned across to Billy. "You'll probably be wanting to change desks soon, won't you?"

"I don't want to move anywhere," Billy muttered, confused.

"Yes, you do," Gerard said, smiling.

"I do?"

Stephanie glared across at Gerard, but he didn't seem to notice.

In fact, Gerard hardly seemed to notice Stephanie at all after that moment.

2 CHAPTER TWO

Over the next few days, Gerard did everything he could think of to get Sadie's attention, from being first to answer questions in class to excelling on the sports field even more than usual. It was, however, wasted effort, because Sadie kept pretty much to herself and remained at her desk down in front, even though Billy — much to everyone's surprise — moved over to the desk next to Rosco.

She seemed to be a very private person and, even though some of the girls tried to get her to join in their games during lunch break and after school, she always politely refused.

Once, Gerard even introduced himself, but she just stared at him with those deep, dark eyes and didn't say anything.

She just doesn't know who I am yet, Gerard thought to himself. She'll soon change her tune when she's a little wiser.

Sadie obviously had her own ideas about who she wanted to be friends with, however, and it certainly wasn't Gerard. To everyone's amazement, she started to be seen with Rosco.

The two of them would have lunch together, hang around the library exchanging books they'd read, and every now and then they'd set up a chessboard during recess and sit there concentrating on the playing

14

pieces, their arms snaking out occasionally to make a move or steal a pawn, castle, or knight. They never appeared to finish a game, not that anyone at school really knew enough about chess to tell; and whenever they set up the board the pieces would be all over it, as if they had started one marathon game and it was going to go on forever.

Strangely enough, it was the chess game that annoyed Gerard the most, as it seemed to involve the two of them completely.

His relationships had always been a little shallow and one-sided, with Gerard being the focus of everything. Anyone else was just there to make him look better.

The more Gerard saw Sadie and Rosco concentrating over their board, moving the pieces and laughing excitedly when one of them made an especially clever move, the more irate he became, stewing over the fact that he had been overlooked for a four-eyed, chess-playing, computer-literate nerd.

He would, he vowed to himself, get his revenge, and by doing so show Rosco up for the jerk he was and make Sadie think twice about cutting him down again.

Gerard was so steamed up he was in danger of going ballistic. And when he came into class one morning to find that Billy had moved back to his old desk and Sadie was now happily occupying the one next to Rosco, everyone knew that something unpleasant was about to happen.

The class sat there and waited to see what Gerard was going to do, but if they were expecting fireworks they were disappointed. He paused at the doorway, slowly looked around the classroom (as if he was inspecting his territory), registered the fact that certain people had moved, and strode majestically to his desk at the back of the room.

Billy bobbed up and down excitedly, glad to be back next to his hero.

"Hey there," he burbled. "Bet you're surprised to see me back? Lucky thing Sadie wanted to move across next to Rosco, huh? She's a funny one, that Sadie. Imagine wanting to sit next to that little creep!"

Gerard ignored Billy and thoughtfully scribbled something on a piece of notepaper, which he then folded, stapled together, and wrote a name on the front. Giving his best smile, he passed the note across to Stephanie and asked her to pass it on.

Even though Stephanie wasn't talking to Gerard at the time, when he smiled people had a habit of doing whatever he asked.

Gradually the note made its way to

Rosco, who read it, looked back over his shoulder at Gerard, and nodded happily.

"What!" Billy exclaimed. "You're not hanging out with him, too, are you?"

"Hardly," Gerard replied with a particularly evil smile. "But if you don't believe me, come on down to the oval at lunchtime. I'm going to teach Rosco something about chess."

"You don't know how to play chess," Billy said.

"You'd be surprised," Gerard half muttered to himself.

3 CHAPTER THREE

At lunchtime the oval was always a scene of chaos, with groups playing football or baseball or hockey; others sitting around having lunch; people running, walking, reading; food fights, real fights, play fights, and fights between friends that could have been either. And though teachers were prepared to patrol through all this, they had no intention whatsoever of attempting to keep order. It was a sort of no-go area for them, and students could easily have committed murder there without being caught.

The oval was a free zone for all sorts of obnoxious behavior, with everyone conspiring against the teachers (and perhaps even the teachers conspiring among themselves) to ensure that whatever happened went undetected.

If you were beaten up by someone on the oval, you went back to the oval the next day to sort it out, or you stayed away forever. It was where student justice — no matter what form it took — was meted out.

Along the far edge of the oval from the school there was a long thicket of trees. Even though it was out of the school grounds, students had been known to meet there to carry out activities that they felt were perhaps even too much for the oval itself. And it was toward this thicket that Gerard, Billy, and Rosco casually strolled that lunchtime.

Gerard and Billy were deep in conversation while Rosco carried his set of chess pieces, which rattled noisily inside their box as he bumped along to the side, and slightly behind, the two larger boys.

Rosco was rather pleased with himself. Life seemed to be taking a better turn for him since Sadie arrived at school. Not only had he made an especially gorgeous and intriguing friend, the two boys in class who had always picked on him and made his life miserable seemed to have suddenly developed an interest in chess. Chess was something he could talk to them about, explaining rules and strategies, and he was looking forward to reaching the shade of the trees and setting up the game.

He was a little nervous about the fact that

neither boy had really said anything to him since they'd left the classroom, but Gerard's note had said to meet them at the trees and to bring his chess set.

Sadie had looked at him very strangely when he said he'd have to cancel their usual game, but Rosco was far too preoccupied to notice. And Sadie had this habit of looking strangely at anything she didn't quite agree with. Rosco had always found her to be friendly and as happy as anyone else he knew when things were going the way she wanted them to, but the moment they didn't she'd get this weird look in her eyes, almost as if there were something or someone else suddenly looking out at him; someone a lot older, who you really didn't want to upset. But this was his big chance to make friends with the people everyone wanted to be friends with, and he wasn't going to mess it up, no matter how disapproving Sadie looked.

"We'll catch up with our game this afternoon," he'd called over his shoulder as he rushed off toward the oval, leaving Sadie staring suspiciously after him.

They finally reached the trees, and after a few seconds of checking to see that no teacher was watching — this involved not really looking back toward the oval, just in case a teacher caught your eye, but sneaking looks quickly over your shoulder and sauntering about attempting to look nonchalant, which basically meant you looked highly suspect — the three of them suddenly disappeared into the shade of the greenery.

Wandering deep into the thicket, the boys passed by the remains of other student excursions into this area. There were plastic bags from lunches going back to prehistoric times, soda cans (some rusted, some still brightly colored), scraps of paper, and the odd, ratty gym shoe. There was even an old school bag that had been there so long it had faded to a white, stiff piece of canvas that was so delicate it would have crumbled at a touch. The smell of eucalyptus leaves and hot, dry sand filled the air.

They found a small clearing that had a fallen tree trunk in the middle and Rosco quickly set about putting chess pieces on the board, prattling away to the other boys in his excitement and nervousness.

"This really is an exciting game, you guys. It's been played by all the great people throughout history, especially generals and political strategists. It's sort of like mathematics, but with a fun element thrown in. You're really going to enjoy it. Once you get the hang of it, that is. The rules and the pieces are easy to learn; it's the actual thinking behind the game that's the hard part. You've got to be able to plan ahead, to anticipate what the other player is thinking, then out-think him . . . or her."

Rosco giggled uncertainly. "Sadie's actually really good at chess. She can plan so far ahead, I have a lot of trouble keeping up."

He finally got the whole game set up and, picking up one of the smallest pieces, turned around to look at Gerard and Billy.

"This," he said, waving the tiny, carved piece of wood in the air, "is a pawn. It's like a foot soldier."

Gerard smiled. Billy did, too, but only because Gerard did — he didn't actually know what was happening.

"And this," said Gerard, producing a small tube from his pocket with a flourish, "is superglue."

Rosco's excited face slowly developed a puzzled frown.

Billy started to snicker and rub his hands down the sides of his jeans as if he was wiping perspiration from his palms.

4 CHAPTER FOUR

After the end-of-lunch bell sounded, students raced back into the classroom, hurtling in a stream through the doorway and spreading out rapidly to their assigned places in a riot of noise, color, and movement. Gerard and Billy returned to their seats, nudging each other and giggling to themselves, except when they passed Sadie, at which time they assumed serious expressions, which dissolved into outright laughter after they were out of her line of sight.

Sadie stared after them, a question on her face, then looked across at Rosco's empty desk.

There was a sudden explosion as Ms. Jenkins slammed a book onto her desk and the class fell silent. She looked out across the classroom, silently counting to make sure everyone was there. Her eyes fell on the empty place where Rosco had been sitting that morning.

"Anybody seen young Rosco?" she queried.

Everybody shook their heads, including Gerard and Billy. Sadie glared back at them, then slowly started to raise her arm.

"Yes, Sadie?" Ms. Jenkins asked.

Just as Sadie opened her mouth to speak, the door of the classroom flew open and a hideous, crazed figure came stumbling into view. It was dressed pretty much like the rest of them, but that was where the resemblance ended.

Instead of a head, it had a mass of black-and-white polyps that jiggled about as it moved, and its hands, which it was waving around frantically, were similarly disfigured. It was making a strange gurgling noise, like a cross between a blocked drain and a whistling kettle, and it crashed into the desks at the front of the room, upending books and scattering students before it like leaves from a high wind.

People were screaming and panicking, running in all directions to get away from this monster that had suddenly appeared among them. Ms. Jenkins stood frozen with her hands clutched in front of her face, as if she were trying to chew all her fingernails at the same time, her eyes wide with fright, as the figure stumbled closer to her.

There were only three people in the room who still appeared in control: Gerard and Billy, who were laughing their heads off, and Sadie, who stared back at them, face blank, her eyes so dark they could have been carved from volcanic rock.

Eventually the crazed figure crashed into Ms. Jenkins's desk and fell to the floor whimpering. The teacher gave a mouselike squeak and, gathering what courage she had left, peered over the desk at the monstrous thing, which was now thrashing about rather pathetically on the floor.

"What? Who?" Ms. Jenkins whispered, almost to herself.

"It's me," croaked the figure. "It's Rosco."

"ROSCO!" she thundered, suddenly snapping out of her state of terror. "WHAT'S THE MEANING OF THIS RIDICULOUS DISPLAY?"

"I . . . uh . . . glue . . ." came the strangely distorted reply.

Ms. Jenkins came hurtling around the desk and grabbed Rosco by his ear, which was now actually two white pawns and a rook, and hauled him to his feet.

"You're in deep, deep trouble, young man," hissed the teacher.

Now that everything had calmed down a bit, everyone could easily see that the monster was really Rosco, only he'd somehow managed to get his entire chess set stuck all over his face and hands. His nose was the white king, his cheeks were adorned with knights and bishops, the black king stuck out of his forehead like a unicorn horn, and every other single chess piece had found a home somewhere on his skin.

It looked like he had, over lunchtime, caught some hideous form of chicken pox.

"Nasty rash you've got there, Rosco," Gerard called from the back of the class, and everyone burst into peals of laughter as Ms. Jenkins hauled the hapless Rosco out through the door and down to the principal's office.

Gerard looked across at Sadie and gave a huge wink and a smile.

Sadie just stared at him, and after a few seconds he experienced a cold shiver and an attack of goose bumps, which his mother had always told him meant that someone had just walked over his grave.

5 CHAPTER FIVE

Gerard and Billy spent the weekend down at the pool, boasting about their little trick with Rosco and the superglue. Everyone thought it was a real hoot, except, of course, Rosco, who no one had seen since Ms. Jenkins dragged him off to see the principal on Friday, and Sadie, who never seemed to go down to the pool anyway.

Their nasty little trick had elevated them to almost folk hero status among those that knew. Gerard now thought he was so hot he was almost ready to go supernova.

Monday dawned bright and clear and, surprising no one, hot.

The students dragged themselves into class, most with their clothes already clinging to them from the heat. It was already well up into the 90s and it had just turned nine o'clock. Nobody was looking forward to a day cooped up inside with only a fan blowing hot, sweat-soaked air back at them and flies droning in and out of the open windows, sticking to their faces and trying to burrow into their ears and eyes.

The appearance of Rosco, however, brightened the mood considerably. He looked like some character from a Hollywood movie who'd been out in a desert too long, with his face a strange, rubbed red color and darker, painful-looking patches where chunks of skin seemed to have disappeared. He walked to his desk with his head down, ignoring the laughter and comments from his classmates.

"I am nosh an animal," Billy slurred, dragging himself around the room doing his well-worn Elephant Man impression. "I'm a shuman being."

"I'm nosh a shuman being," slurred Gerard, close on Billy's tail. "I'm a Roshcanimal."

Etc, etc . . .

Rosco kept his head down and pretended to read a chemistry textbook, but his already red color deepened throughout the proceedings.

It only calmed down after Ms. Jenkins made her appearance, which was even sweatier and more bedraggled than her students.

"She sweats a lot, don't you think?" Billy whispered across to Gerard.

"All adults sweat a lot, in case you haven't noticed. They've got bigger pores or something."

"I thought they had hands like the rest of us," muttered Billy, looking rather puzzled.

There were times when Gerard really despaired about his friend's command of the English language.

"Enough whispering," Ms. Jenkins called wearily. "After the excitement of Friday afternoon and Rosco's attempt to frighten us all to death, I'd like this week to be a little more self-contained, thank you very much. As you'll all be able to tell from Rosco's appearance, sticking things to your anatomy with glue can be detrimental to your health, not to mention your skin tone, so please, everyone, let's have a quiet, relaxed time with our books. It's too hot to do anything else. Please turn to page two hundred and twelve of your biology text. This morning's session will be on the human skin, in honor of our scabby friend over there."

Rosco shrank even lower down in his desk than normal.

After lunch that day, things in the classroom had changed a little.

Gerard had noticed Sadie and Stephanie chatting together in the oval, which was unusual, since Sadie rarely, if ever, talked to anyone except Rosco. And when he got back to class after lunch he found that Sadie was now in Stephanie's seat, the two of them having swapped seats while everyone was sweating it out in the heat.

Gerard was delighted. It seemed that his little trick with Rosco was paying dividends already. As his entire reason for treating Rosco so badly had been to get Sadie's attention, it now seemed that he wouldn't have to continue with his vendetta, the desired result having already occurred.

Sadie, however, avoided his eye all through the afternoon, and no amount of winks, pssssts, or hurried coughs could get her to look in his direction. She's just playing hard to get, Gerard thought as he packed up his books that afternoon; things will be different tomorrow.

Unlike everyone else in the class that afternoon, Sadie seemed to have an awful lot of work to complete, and she stayed at her desk after the others had filed out of the classroom. The stuffy room hadn't seemed to bother her all that much, and she seemed happy flicking through the pages of various books and taking down notes.

"Make sure you're ready to go by the time the cleaners come by, Sadie," Ms. Jenkins said as she left for home. "We don't want you locked up in here all night, do we?"

"No, Ms. Jenkins," Sadie replied, hardly even glancing up from the page she was reading.

"Are you sure it's not too hot in here for you?" Ms. Jenkins continued. She was un-used to students staying behind to work after hours and was worried that something might be wrong.

This time Sadie looked up and smiled.

"Oh, no, Ms., I like the heat. Reminds me a bit of Haiti. I can take about as much of this as the weather can dish out. The hotter it gets the better I feel."

Ms. Jenkins nodded slowly and walked out into the heat, which was so strong it felt as if she were walking through the door of a furnace.

" 'Bye, then, Sadie. See you tomorrow."

"Good-bye, Ms."

As soon as the teacher had gone, Sadie slowly turned her head and looked across at Gerard's desk. Her eyes appeared to glitter, as if there was a small spark somewhere deep inside her, and a smile tweaked the corners of her mouth. She let out a long, slow breath and closed her eyes.

CHAPTER SIX

That night, Gerard fell asleep on top of his sheets, covered in sweat, and woke up a couple of hours later shivering, his skin crawling with goose bumps.

First he pulled his sheet up over himself, but that didn't seem to make any difference, so he went to his closet and found the one ragged, hardly used blanket that was kept there. Gerard could never remember having used the blanket in his entire life, but he certainly felt a need for it now. He pulled it over himself and lay there waiting to warm up, but it didn't seem to make any difference, so he pulled on a couple of T-shirts and his sweatpants as well.

"What's got into you, Gerard," his mother exclaimed when she came in to wake him up for school. "It's boiling outside and you've got so many clothes on, you look like the Michelin man."

All Gerard could do by way of reply was chatter his teeth.

"Oh, you poor dear," said his mother. "Have you got a fever or something?"

She came over and put her hand to his brow.

"Your temperature's quite normal," she said, frowning. Then she suddenly looked angry. "If you want to get out of going to school you'll have to be a bit more inventive than that. Now get out of bed, out of all

50

those clothes, and come and have some breakfast this instant."

Gerard's teeth were chattering so much while he ate his cornflakes he thought he was going to bite the end off his spoon, but his mother refused to believe there was anything wrong with him.

"You'll have to do better than that, Gerard, my boy, before I'll keep you home from school. You gave me such a fright this morning, I have a good mind to ground you for a week."

Gerard knew better than to argue with his mother, especially when she thought he'd been faking being sick.

When he left home that morning, however, he snuck a sweater and long pants into his bag, which he put on when he was out of sight of the house, and he was wearing as many T-shirts as he could without making his mother suspicious.

He didn't know what was happening to him, but in the back of his mind he had the stirrings of an idea as to why.

People looked at him very strangely when he got to school, especially since Gerard was always known for his impeccable dress sense and the fact that he liked to wear things that would show off his good build. This morning, however, he looked like he'd dressed in a Salvation Army bin.

"Nice outfit," snickered Billy when Gerard took his seat in class.

"Shut your face, brain death," Gerard hissed, without even looking across at Billy, "otherwise I'll stuff your head and shoulders down the crap trap at recess."

Billy gulped loudly and didn't look over at Gerard all morning. He knew better than to annoy him when he was angry and he was certainly angry about something. Billy hoped it wasn't something he'd done.

Gerard seemed to get angrier and angrier as the morning progressed, rifling around through his desk and muttering to himself, though Billy couldn't quite work out what he was saying. From the sound of it, though, Gerard had lost something. And from the way he kept looking over and glaring at Sadie, it appeared as if he thought she'd taken whatever it was he'd lost.

Sadie didn't appear to notice, though, and just kept working away with a tiny smile flickering at the corners of her mouth.

"Someone's gone and taken four of my pens," Gerard said accusingly at Billy while they were sitting down in the oval eating.

"I wouldn't be worried about your pens, buddy. It's the shaking I'd be worried about."

"I'm not shaking, you twerp. I'm shivering."

"I'd still be worried. You're all dressed up like you're living in Antarctica or something. What's the matter with you?"

"Nothing," Gerard snarled. "I've just caught a chill or something."

"You've caught a chill in 110-degree heat?"

"Yes, I've caught a chill." Gerard tossed his hardly touched bologna sandwiches to one side.

"Why don't you go see a doctor?" Billy said, eyeing Gerard's discarded lunch.

"Because my mom thinks I'm faking it to get out of going to school."

"Been done."

"I know that. Eat the sandwiches if you want."

Billy snatched them up before Gerard changed his mind.

"Thanks, pal."

"I think that Sadie did it," Gerard said, staring across the oval to where Rosco and Sadie were playing chess.

"What, gave you a chill?"

"No, idiot," Gerard snapped, "stole my pens!"

"Oh, riiiight."

7

CHAPTER SEVEN

$\mathbb{T}$hat night Gerard was so cold he took every single piece of clothing he had out of his dresser and put it on top of his bed.

"Gerard, you're an idiot," his mother said when she came into his room in the morning and found him shivering under the pile of clothes. "You can't possibly think this little charade of yours is going to work."

"But Mom, I'm COLD!" he shouted.

"You don't feel it and you don't look it, so

stop this nonsense right now or your father's going to hear about it."

In the shower he turned the hot water all the way up, but it didn't seem to make one iota of difference.

That day, Gerard discovered that his pencil case and eraser were missing from his desk as well.

"Has anyone seen any of Gerard's things?" Ms. Jenkins asked when Gerard mentioned his loss.

The entire class shook their heads, though Gerard was sure he saw Sadie smile.

"You see," Ms. Jenkins said to him, "you've just misplaced them. No one would steal anything like that from you, Gerard. Everyone has their own things, so there's no reason for them to take yours."

"Yeah, I bet," he mumbled under his breath as he walked back to his desk.

"What was that, Gerard?"

"Nothing, Ms."

Each night, Gerard got colder (though the cold seemed to lose its edge during the day, until by late afternoon he was almost feeling himself again), and every day that week he found something else missing from his desk.

By now he was certain it was Sadie taking his things, because the more stuff that disappeared, the happier she seemed to be. He couldn't quite work out how his feeling cold fit into everything, but he was sure it was all connected.

The final straw was Friday morning.

Gerard opened his desk to find that someone had cleaned it.

His books were still there and everything, but it looked like someone had gone through with a small broom and dusted away all the usual inside-of-desk debris. There was no dust, no pencil shavings, no chewed-off pieces of fingernail. Someone had even gone to the trouble of removing all the stray hairs from his comb.

Gerard glared at Sadie.

This time she grinned openly at him.

With a large, visible shiver, Gerard began to plan his revenge.

"It's Sadie," Gerard chattered to Billy that day in the oval. "She's stealing my things and using them to make me cold."

"Oh, pull the other one, Gerard, it plays 'Jingle Bells,'" Billy said, laughing out loud. "How can someone make you cold by stealing your pens?"

"*And* my eraser *and* the dust from my desk *and* the hairs from my comb!"

"Maybe she's got a 'thing' for you. Like these stalkers, you know, who follow movie stars around and rummage through their trash cans and steal their used tea bags and stuff?"

"Like that guy who was after Madonna?"

"Yeah, like that."

"Nah. It's got something to do with what we did to Rosco."

"She hasn't stolen anything of mine, and I stuck as many chess pieces on him as you did."

"But it was my idea."

"So?"

"So it was *my* idea. She's going after the brains."

"Thanks very much."

"Don't mention it."

"What are you going to do?" said Billy sulkily.

"What *we're* going to do, Billy, old buddy, is sneak over to her place tonight and teach her a lesson. Make her stop doing whatever it is she's doing."

"And just exactly what is it that she's doing, Gerard?"

"I'm not sure yet," said Gerard thoughtfully. "But I'm going to find out tonight when we go and get my hair back."

"You're going to get your hair back?"

"And some of hers." Gerard gave an evil smile and made a snipping motion with his fingers. Billy's mouth opened wide.

"You're not serious. You're not going to cut her hair off?"

"You betcha," said Gerard, still grinning. "She's really proud of all that hair and beads and stuff. It'll serve her right, after what she's been doing to me."

"Well, you can do it yourself," said Billy, getting up and walking away from his friend. "I'm not having anything to do with that. That's just plain stupid. And you don't even really know if she's doing anything."

"But she's using magic or something on me, Billy. I thought we were friends. You've got to help me."

"Magic, my foot. You can go to hell, Gerard."

Billy kept walking up toward the classrooms without looking back at Gerard, who shouted after him, "OH, THANKS VERY MUCH, BILLY!"

"Don't mention it," Billy mumbled. Gerard couldn't see the half smile he had on his face.

CHAPTER EIGHT

After dinner that night, Gerard went off to his room early, pleading homework and fatigue. He lay in his bed shivering until he heard his parents turn out the lights and retire for the evening.

Fully clothed, he hopped out of bed, removed the screen and snuck silently out his window.

He was dressed in his black sweatsuit and black Nikes and wore a black baseball cap on his head. The night was hot and sticky, but Gerard shivered as he slipped through the dark, silent streets of Xanthers toward the old Catchpole house at the end of town.

In his pocket he carried his mother's dress-making shears, which he took out occasionally, opening and closing them so he could hear the satisfying scrape of metal on metal. He could imagine them snipping through Sadie's dark tresses, almost hear the sound of her beaded braids hitting the floor.

Gerard was excited and, even though he was still so cold he felt like he had icicles for bones, he felt that some of his shivers were those of anticipation.

When he finally arrived at Sadie's house, he found it in almost complete darkness. There was, however, a dull, flickering light coming from one of the bedroom windows.

On silent, sneakered feet, Gerard crept

along the side of the house, ducking under the windowsills just in case someone was peering out of the darkness.

The closer he got to the flickering light, the colder he felt, until he thought his chattering teeth could be heard by anyone living in the houses nearby. All remained silent, however, and Gerard finally reached the window and eased his head up over the sill to peer inside. In his left hand he held his mother's shears.

What greeted Gerard was not a scene that he was expecting.

The light in the room was coming from several large candles that were positioned in a ring on the floor of the bedroom. Sadie was sitting inside the ring of light with her back to the window. She was wearing a strange, old-fashioned white dress covered in bows and flounces, and the candlelight made her dark skin contrast vividly against the white dress. There were no braids in her hair and it was scattered about her shoulders in wild disarray.

The window was open and had no screen and Gerard could hear her chanting softly to herself, and she'd occasionally give out a half-subdued chuckle of glee.

All around the room there were strange, ugly little statues and masks, each of which looked as if it'd come straight from the set of a Mortal Kombat video game.

I knew it was some sort of magic, Gerard thought; and, just as he was about to lift himself up over the windowsill and into the room, Sadie's chanting got slightly louder.

She rose up off the floor, held something over her head in both hands, and started to walk around inside the ring of light. On the floor in the middle of the candles was an old plastic ice-cream container.

Sadie's hair was all over her face, so Gerard couldn't see her eyes, but he could clearly see what it was she was holding over her head. It was a weird doll made out of all the things that were missing from his desk. The body was made out of his pencil case, the arms and legs were the missing pens, and the head was made from his eraser and had tiny eyes and a mouth drawn on it. When the candlelight flared slightly, he could make out what looked like pencil shavings and hair stuck all over the doll.

Gerard could see waves of heat coming from Sadie's body, like those you see rising from a road on a really hot day. He crouched down to see what would happen next.

After circling the ice-cream container a few times, chanting rhythmically while she did, she held the doll up high over her head and plunged it down into the container.

Two things happened simultaneously: First, Gerard was sure he heard the distinctive sound of ice cubes and water as Sadie plunged the doll into the container; and second, Gerard was hit by such an intense wave of cold that it brought a loud, painful groan from his lips.

Sadie immediately leaped back from the container, flicking her hair back from her face as she did, glaring toward the window. What Gerard saw brought more than a moan from his lips.

Gerard shrieked from way, way down inside himself.

Sadie's eyes looked like they were on fire, blazing out from her face, and her teeth were bared in a primitive, feral snarl. She was a horror movie come to life, and Gerard's feet simply couldn't move fast enough.

He let go of the windowsill and ran as if every demon he could ever imagine were on his heels, the breath pumping out of his chest like steam from an old train smoke-stack.

Inside the room, Sadie grinned to herself and picked up the container. The doll was half submerged in ice water, the cubes bobbing around like prefabricated icebergs.

She walked slowly through the house to the kitchen, where she gave out a tiny chuckle, opened the door to the freezer, and placed the container and doll inside.

Then she went off to bed.

9 CHAPTER NINE

For Gerard, the run back to his house proved to be the longest in his life. The farther he ran, the slower he got, the cold eating into him like some untreatable disease. He could feel it clinging to him, creeping in through his skin as he ran, his muscles literally freezing as he tried to move. His bones felt like cold lead, and each step became harder and harder to manage.

By the time he reached the front path to his house he was hardly moving at all, and it took him close to fifteen minutes just to reach the front door.

Unlike his body, his brain was racing at the speed of light. . . . "Got to get home. . . . Got to get home. . . . Got to get warm. . . . Got to find my parents. . . ."

He reached out his hand, lifting it agonizingly slowly toward the doorbell, which, to his panicked mind, would bring his parents and safety, but he didn't quite make it.

His finger was exactly one millimeter from the bell when everything except Gerard's brain froze solid.

And that was how his father found him when he went outside at six the next morning to see if the newspaper had arrived: frozen solid with a look of absolute terror on his face.

Gerard became something of a celebrity after that, not to mention a medical phenomenon. You see, according to every doctor and specialist his parents took the frozen figure to, there was nothing medically wrong with him.

Gerard's heart was beating and his brain patterns appeared quite normal. He just couldn't move. Nothing anyone did could get any single portion of his body to change from that bizarre posture he was in when his father found him.

Finally, his parents took him home and stuck him in the corner of the living room, where they used to chat to him at night "just in case he can hear us."

He did thaw out eventually. Exactly one year to the day from the time he froze and, coincidentally, on the same day that Sadie and her family left Xanthers and the electricity was turned off in the old Catchpole house.

Gerard wasn't his old self, however.

In fact, Gerard was a different person entirely.

He was nice to people, for starters. Polite even. And he and Billy became good friends with Rosco.

The girls still thought he was pretty hot, but it was in a different way. You could almost say that Gerard became "nice."

After all, he'd had a lot of time to think about his behavior.

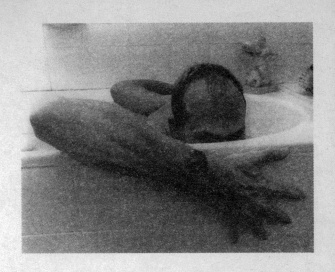

S.R. MARTIN

S.R. Martin was born and grew up in the beachside suburbs of Perth, Australia. A fascination with the ocean led to an early career in marine biology, but this was cut short when he decided the specimens he collected looked better under an orange-and-cognac sauce than they did under a microscope. After even quicker careers in banking, teaching, and journalism, a wanderlust led him through most of Australia's capital cities and then on to periods of time living in Hong Kong, Taiwan, South Korea, the United Kingdom, and the United States. Returning to Australia, he settled for Melbourne and a career as a freelance writer. In addition to the Insomniacs series, S.R. Martin is the author of *Swampland*, coming soon from Scholastic.